This Book Belongs to:

Santa
Are You For Real?

Harold Myra

ILLUSTRATED BY JANE KURISU

Tommy
NELSON™

Thomas Nelson, Inc.

Nashville

Copyright © 1979, 1997 by Harold Myra

Illustrations copyright © 1997 by Tommy Nelson™, a division of Thomas Nelson, Inc.

Published in Nashville, Tennessee, by Tommy Nelson™, a division of Thomas Nelson, Inc.

Scripture quotation is from the *International Children's Bible, New Century Version*,
copyright © 1986, 1988, 1999 by Tommy Nelson™, a division of Thomas Nelson, Inc.

Library of Congress Cataloging-in-Publication Data

Myra, Harold Lawrence, 1939–

    Santa, are you for real? / Harold Myra : illustrated by Jane Kurisu
        p. cm.
    Summary: Convinced that Santa Claus does not exist, Todd learns the true facts from his father.
    ISBN 0-8499-1492-2
    1. Santa Claus—Juvenile fiction. [1. Santa Claus—Fiction. 2. Christmas—Fiction. 3. Stories
in rhyme.] I. Kurisu, Jane, ill. II. Title.
    PZ8.M997San   1997   97-25497
    [E]—dc21   CIP
                                                               AC

Printed in China

06 07 PHX 9 8

A Note to Parents

Christmas, children, and Santa Claus. The combination often generates adult explosions against materialism. Why should children be encouraged to be so self-centered, so caught up with a myth that distorts Christmas into a pagan holiday?

Why indeed? I had always been ambivalent myself. But then I read about the historic Saint Nicholas. Even after skimming off the tall tales and adjusting for medieval exaggeration, he comes off as a rather exciting person for children to know about. It's important to understand the roots of the Santa Claus phenomenon and how the original Saint Nick put the Christ Child clearly at the heart of his Christmas.

—Harold Myra

'Twas the night before Christmas,
and out on the street,
a wee boy was standing,
big boots on his feet.

He stamped them and kicked them,
threw snow at a rock
to crowd out the songs
of the kids on the block.

"Hey, hey, hey," he heard them say,

"Santa's phony—all the way!

Hey! No way, a flying sleigh!"

Dad watched Todd come in,
saw his face was all glum,
~~so~~ he bent down and asked,
"What's the matter, old chum?"

"No Santa or reindeer will
come to our place!
The chimney's too skinny.
He can't really fly.
He's not at the North Pole.
It's all a big lie."

Dad reached for the boy,
pulled him tight to his side,
and kissed him and told him,
"Let's see, Todd, who's lied."

Saint Nicholas was a real person. He lived about 300 years after Jesus was born. He loved Jesus very much.

One favorite story about him goes like this:

Nicholas loved to give gifts, especially to the poor. Only he gave them secretly because he wasn't looking for thanks.

Nick knew a kind but poor man with three lovely daughters who all wanted to get married. But in those days, a woman had to have money—a dowry—before a wedding could be announced.

When Nick heard about this, he put some money into a bag and, while it was dark, walked to their house.

He tossed the money into the oldest daughter's room, and it fell into a stocking hung there to dry. Nick quietly left.

The oldest daughter had a marvelous wedding.

Later, on another night, Nick did the same thing for the second daughter.

But who had helped them? they wondered.

One daughter was left. Would someone give her a dowry too?

Not too long after that Nick sneaked up to her house and tossed in a third bag of gold. But this time the father heard him! Nick realized he had been seen and tried to dash away. But the father ran and caught up to him.

The father recognized Nick and smiled.

"Keep my secret," Nick asked.

And the father did.

For years after that, no one knew who had helped the three daughters.

And because Nick loved Jesus, he kept doing kind things for people.

After he died, people called him a saint.

And over the years, people remembered Saint Nicholas and how he gave gifts.

In Holland they call him Sinterclaas. In England they call him Father Christmas. In France he is called Père Nöel. In the United States he is called Santa Claus.

The real Saint Nicholas is now in heaven with Jesus. When you see a Santa in a store or a parade, think of Saint Nick.

Of course some children know all about Santa and presents and reindeer but forget all about Jesus. For Saint Nick, that would ruin Christmas! Jesus was Nick's whole life.

Saint Nicholas gave gifts because Jesus came on the first Christmas to give himself for us.

Todd said, "I'm going to do
what Nick was about,
I'm going to give gifts
and not be found out!"

Todd ran up the stairs,
his face full of scheming.
A long time went by
till he came back all beaming.

Stuffed toys and a dump truck,
a clown with one leg
all wrapped for Michelle
and her brother Greg.

Todd piled them up high
by the tree lighted bright,
and then he announced,
"Saint Nick's here tonight!"

"I'll act like Saint Nick," Todd said to his dad.
"It's Jesus he loved—He makes us all glad!"

His dad just laughed as he lifted the boy.
"That's wonderful, Todd.
To share gives us joy."

As the family sat around
and talked half the night,
Todd thought he saw,
in the snow and
moonlight . . .

...a bright-eyed Saint Nicholas
with his sack looking in,
and wide across his face,
a jolly old grin.